MARC BROWN

What a Mess!

D.W. opened the front door. "Grandma Thora's here!" she yelled.

"Thanks for coming over," said Dad.

Grandma Thora took Kate from Dad's arms. "You're welcome," she said.

"Everybody's acting so weird," said D.W. "I haven't seen Mom or Dad for a gazillion hours."

"Your mom is working really hard," said Grandma Thora. "It's tax time. And your dad has a big party to cater."

"Will you play with me?" asked D.W.

"I'd love to," said Grandma Thora.

D.W. played her drum for Grandma Thora. "Want to hear it again?" she asked.

"No thanks, D.W.," said Grandma Thora. "I have a headache."

"I can help you," said D.W. She ran to get her doctor's bag.

D.W. tapped Grandma Thora's knee with a plastic hammer. "It's a headache, all right," she said. "You need some rest."

"And don't worry," said D.W. "I can handle everything. Just sit back and watch Crazy Bus."

Mom was trying to work when Arthur and D.W. ran into her office.

"Arthur, take off those dirty shoes," said D.W.

"What?" asked Arthur.

"I'm in charge," said D.W. "And you need to clean your room."

"Moooooooooooom!" called Arthur.

"You two will have to work it out," said Mom.

"But Dad!" pleaded Arthur.

"Have to go, or I'll be late," Dad said. "We can talk when I get back."

"I'm older," said Arthur. "So if anybody is in charge around here, it's me."

"Oh, no, you don't," said D.W. "I thought of it first."

Arthur rolled his eyes and sat down next to his grandmother.

"Maybe Bionic Bunny is on," said Grandma Thora.

"Right!" said Arthur. "And it's a brand-new episode."

But the moment the show started, so did the vacuum cleaner.

"I can't hear the TV," shouted Arthur.

"What?" shouted D.W.

"I can't hear!" yelled Arthur.

"I can't hear, either," D.W. yelled.

A short while later, the phone rang.

"D.W., it's for you," called Arthur.

Arthur waited until D.W. picked up the phone. Then he started the vacuum.

"Arthur, I can't hear," shouted D.W.

"Did you say something?" shouted Arthur.

D.W. took the phone into the closet.

"We need to do some laundry," D.W. said, looking at his dirty clothes.

"It's *my* uniform," said Arthur. "I'll wash it."

"You can't wash everything together," warned D.W.

Arthur tossed his uniform into the washer and added detergent.

"You need more soap," said D.W.

And when Arthur wasn't watching,
D.W. added more soap—lots more soap.

Soon soap bubbles overflowed from the washing machine and covered the floor.

"You messed up," said D.W., giggling.

"You mop up," said Arthur. "I have to take out the trash."

"*You* mop," said D.W. "*I'll* take out the trash."

"The trash is my job," argued Arthur.

Arthur tried to grab the trash bag, but he slipped and fell on the wet floor.

"Better clean this up," said D.W. "Somebody might slip."

Arthur watched D.W. take the trash outside.

"You forgot to put the lid on the can," Arthur yelled.

A few minutes later, D.W. looked out the window.

"There goes your dopey dog running around with an ice cream carton on his head," said D.W.

"Oh, no," groaned Arthur.

A little while later, Arthur went to check on Grandma Thora.

"Need anything?" he asked.

"No, thank you, Arthur," said Grandma Thora.

"Anything *I* can do for you?" asked D.W.

"No, thank you, D.W.," said Grandma Thora.

"Just let me know if you change your mind," said Arthur.

"Your teensiest wish is my command," offered D.W.

"On second thought," Grandma Thora replied. "Maybe you two could give Kate her snack. Together."

D.W. ran into the kitchen.
"I know what Kate likes," she said.

"She likes these little orange crackers," said Arthur.

Kate put a handful of crackers in her mouth.

D.W. ignored Arthur. "Look, Kate, it's your favorite," she said. "Crunch cereal."

Kate put a handful of cereal in her mouth.

"She needs raisins," said Arthur, piling them on her tray.

Suddenly there was a loud SPLAT!

Some soggy cereal hit Arthur on the head.

Then gooey crackers and raisins landed in D.W.'s hair.

Kate started to cry.

"Now look what you've done!" cried D.W. "Poor Kate tried to eat everything you gave her!"

"No," said Arthur. "She tried to eat everything *we* gave her.
Now we have to clean up this mess."

Kate stopped crying when Mom and Dad came in.

"What happened?" asked Mom.

"It's a long story," said Arthur.

"It's nice to see you two helping each other," said Mom.
"But maybe you could use *our* help to clean up this mess."

"Okay," said D.W. "But I'm in charge."